Faster! Faster!

by Lea Martin

illustrated by Nancy Coffelt

 HOUGHTON MIFFLIN   BOSTON

Ed was riding a shiny new bike when he went to see his friend Fred.

"Hello, Fred," said Ed, as he spun around Fred.

Ed was a fine biker. Everyone said so.

"I'd like to be able to ride like that!"
said Fred.

"Hop on," said Ed. "I'll show you how."

Fred hopped on the bike, and Ed told him what to do.

"Pedal fast!" shouted Ed. "Faster! Faster!"

Fred pedaled as fast as he could.

But he forgot to look where he was pedaling.

Round and round Fred went, riding until he ended up back where he began. He was getting dizzy.

"You pedaled fast, but you forgot to steer," said Ed. "This time, steer!"

6

Fred remembered to steer, but he forgot to pedal fast.

Slower and slower went the wheels, until the bike was barely moving. Then Fred fell over with a crash!

"I can't do it!" cried Fred. "I'm afraid
I'm a very clumsy fox."

Ed seemed to be thinking, but he was
keeping his thoughts to himself.

8

"I'm going into town," Ed said at last.
"May I come too?" asked Fred.
"Not this time," said Ed. "I'll see you
later." Then he went down the road.

Fred was very sad. Ed never went to town without him before.

"Maybe he doesn't want me for a friend anymore," Fred thought. And he grew sadder and sadder.

Then Fred looked up and saw Ed
coming back. "What's this?" thought Fred.
"Does Ed have two bikes with him or are
my eyes playing tricks on me?"

Ed had a bike made for two!

Ed steered and Fred pedaled. Together the two friends yelled, "Faster! Faster!"

Fred and Ed were fine bikers. Everyone said so.